D0364112

TALES FROM THE DARK SIDE

BLOOD
ON
SNOW

Tim Bowler
Illustrated by Jason Cockroft

For the people of Totnes

TALES FROM THE DARK SIDE

BLOOD ON SNOW

Tim Bowler

Illustrated by Jason Cockroft

Hodder
Children's
Books

a division of Hodder Headline Limited

CONTENTS

1

THE CASTLE

I didn't want to go. I was terrified of the place. But what excuse could I have given to Mr Tucker? Told him I was scared of an old ruin? That would have gone down like a lead balloon.

The trouble is I'm really sensitive to places. Sometimes I'll go somewhere and it'll give me the creeps. I don't always know why. It just does. It's kind of an odd thing so I've always kept quiet about it. I haven't even told Cal or Ellie and they're my best mates.

Mum and Dad have always known about my fears, of course. But I didn't tell them about this latest one. Dad was under big pressure at work. There was a strike on the way and as the union's chief negotiator, he had plenty to think about.

And Mum – well, I wasn't going to tell her. She frets too much about me as it is. Hopefully, I thought, Dad would be too busy worrying about work and Mum would be too busy worrying about him for either of them to notice there was anything wrong with me.

Odette would be different. There was never any fooling her. It's weird having a sister like that. She's only seven but she always seems to spot when I'm having a shivery moment. She'll tell me I've got one of my 'funny faces', as she puts it.

But she can't stop me having these moments. No one can. I just have to face them when they come. And I didn't like the feelings I was getting right now.

'Totnes Castle was built in the early months of 1068,' Mr Tucker was telling the class, his bald head shining in the hot June sun like a bright, crinkly egg. 'It's what's called a motte and bailey castle. The Normans had lots of them built all over the country.'

He beamed round at us.

'This huge mound we're on is called the motte and it's made up of pounded earth and rock. And as you can see from up here on the wall walk, we've got a commanding view over Totnes and the river Dart.'

I glanced warily over the town, feeling more uncomfortable than ever. My family had only been in Totnes for nine months but I'd felt funny about the castle right from the start. I had no wish to be here.

But history teachers like Tucker are driven men. And if you're doing the Norman Conquest in class and there's a Norman castle right on your doorstep, then *you* try standing up and telling him you don't want to go.

He was right about one thing, though. The

wall walk was the highest point of the castle
and it did give you a terrific view of the town
below.

I could see the houses and shops on either
side of the high street and, further down the
hill, the tower of St Mary's Church. To the right
of that was the archway of the old east gate.

And far below, at the bottom of town, I
could make out Totnes Bridge and the river
Dart, licking its way towards the sea like a
huge, grey tongue.

I was just hoping Tucker might cut this lecture short – since it was so hot – when he went blundering on.

'That walled area of grassy land at the base of the motte is what's called the bailey. As you can see, it's now an empty space but in Norman times it would have had lots of things in it. Who can tell me some of the buildings we might have found there?'

'Burger King, sir?' said Cal.

'Very funny, Calvin.'

'Lodgings, sir,' said Ellie.

'Good!' said Tucker. 'What else?'

Silence.

'They'd have had to eat, wouldn't they?'

'A kitchen, sir!' said Gemma.

'Well done, Gemma. What else?'

Another silence.

'Come on,' said Tucker. 'I know it's hot but switch your brains on. There'd have been lots of other buildings in the bailey. The place would have been a hive of activity.'

The only activity I could think of right now was the movement of sweat down my neck. But it wasn't from the heat. It was from the deepening unease I felt as the atmosphere of this place started to work upon me.

Something was wrong here. Something was terribly wrong. But I couldn't pick up what it was. I felt a growing desire to run and keep running, anywhere just as long it was away from this place.

'Still waiting,' said Tucker brightly. 'Yes, Damien?'

'A hall, sir.'

'Good. And?'

'Stables,' said Lawrence.

'Storerooms,' said Melanie.

'That's better,' said Tucker, wiping his forehead. 'And there'd have been other things too, which we'll be talking about later when we get back to school. But let me just tell you a little bit about how the castle has developed over the centuries.'

Again I felt the atmosphere of the place work upon me. The desire to run grew stronger. I felt as though someone I didn't know was close to me, very close, and watching me intently. Yet I could see no one apart from the familiar faces from my class, and Mr Tucker. I looked at him, willing him to take us away from here.

But he went on, unaware of my distress. I tried to push aside my fear by focusing rigidly on what he was saying. He was a good history teacher, as long as you didn't stand too near him when he was in full flow. If you did that, you got caught by the little jets of spit that came whizzing out through the gaps in his teeth.

But even Mr Tucker – with all his enthusiasm – couldn't make Totnes Castle sound anything other than completely boring.

As far as I could tell from what he was saying, nothing exciting had ever happened here in over a thousand years. No one had laid siege to the place, tried to blow it up, take it over or do anything to it. Of all the castles in England, it had to be the one with the sleepiest history. So why was I feeling so frightened?

I glanced round at the rest of the group. They looked hot and tired, though they were all dutifully listening. I caught Cal's eye and forced myself to smile at him. He grinned back. Tucker picked up our little exchange at once.

'Do I have your full attention, Will?'

'Yes, sir,' I answered. 'Motte and bailey castle dating from the early months of 1068.'

'And who had it built?'

'The Normans, sir.'

'Thank you. But pay better attention. You too, Calvin.'

And Tucker went rambling on. But this time I didn't hear a word.

Something had suddenly happened to me.

2

THE SHIVERY PRESENCE

Someone had stepped inside me.

That was the only way to describe it. It was like a shiver that ran through every part of me – my muscles, my bones, my skin, even my brain.

I saw Cal watching me strangely and I could tell he knew something was wrong. The rest of the class went on listening to Tucker and seemed unaware of what was happening to me. I was breathing hard now, my mind on this shivery feeling inside me. Then I heard a voice. It seemed to come from inside my head.

'Help me,' it said.

I stiffened and looked around me. For a moment the old stone walls of the castle seemed to darken, as though a shadow had fallen upon them. What was happening? This was meant to be a bright June morning.

I took a step to the left and to my relief felt the shivery presence leave me. The walls brightened again and I breathed slowly out.

Tucker was telling us to go off and find the things on our worksheets. 'Meet by the gate in half an hour,' he said. And the group split up. Cal came straight over.

'You all right, Will?' he said. 'You went white just now.'

'I'm OK.'

'Are you sure? Your face seemed to sort of change. Almost like you were another person.'

I looked away. That was just how it had felt. Like I was another person. I hoped the shivery presence wouldn't come back.

But it did. Only minutes later. Most of the group, including Cal, had gone down to look at the bailey but I was still up on the wall walk. And there it was again – the cold presence, the urgent voice inside me.

'Help me,' it said.

It was a boy's voice. It sounded like someone about fourteen like me. It even felt like my own voice. But that was daft. My lips weren't moving. Then suddenly – to my horror – they were.

'Help me,' they said. 'Help me.'

'Talking to yourself again, Will?' said Ellie, sauntering past me. She didn't stop and the voice spoke again through my lips.

'Help me.'

The dusky shadow was falling again, this time over the whole town. The outlines of the houses and shops, the east gate, the river Dart – all seemed to tremble and lose their shape. In spite of the heat, a chill started to creep over me. I began to shake. Then I heard another voice.

'Will!'

I turned and saw Cal standing below me in the castle keep. To my relief, the darkness seemed to clear, the heat of the day returned, and the shivery presence slipped away once more. Cal called up again.

'Come on, Will! We're all waiting for you!'

'But Tucker said to meet in half an hour.'

'You've been up there forty-five minutes! I've been sent to get you. Hurry up or you'll cop it!'

I stared down at him. Forty-five minutes? That couldn't be right. Tucker had only told us to wander off a few minutes ago. Or so it felt. I hurried down the steps to join Cal. He glanced at my worksheet and frowned.

'You haven't done any of the tasks,' he said. 'What have you been doing all this time?' He looked me over suddenly. 'You still look white. You sure you're not ill?'

I turned away. I couldn't talk about what had happened, not even to Cal. He'd think I was crazy.

'I'm fine,' I said. 'Come on. Let's go.'

I hurried down the steps to the bailey where the others were waiting by the gate. Tucker gave me a sardonic look.

'Kind of you to join us, Will – eventually.' He glanced round at the others. 'Now can we not dawdle on the way back to school? We're a little bit later leaving than I intended.

Thanks to a certain person.' His eyes flickered in my direction again.

But I was already hurrying towards the gate. I couldn't get out of this place quick enough. Whatever was in there, whatever it was that had taken me over, I wanted to leave it behind at the castle. I wanted it to stay there for good.

But it came with me.

It seemed to walk through my feet, breathe through my breath, think through my thoughts. It whispered and murmured inside me, and its words were coming out through my own mouth.

'He killed them,' I was saying. 'He threw them in the river by the ford.'

Cal and Ellie were walking beside me. I saw them glance at me but my mind was not on them. It was on the dark veil falling once more over the buildings and streets of Totnes. And the chill that came with it.

'Will?' said Cal. 'You're talking to yourself.'

'He was doing that up on the wall walk,' said Ellie.

I tried to respond but found I could not.

'Will?' said Ellie. 'What's happening?'

I heard the fear in her voice. The shivery presence moved inside me but did not go. I heard Cal shout ahead to Mr Tucker.

'Sir! Something's wrong with Will!'

'Have you only just discovered that, Calvin?'

'Sir! It's serious!'

Tucker was with me moments later. He was like a shadow now, just as Cal and Ellie and my classmates had become shadows. And as they closed round, I saw other shadows. The shadows of another life. A life I did not understand and wanted no part of. The voice spoke through me again.

'He killed them. He threw them in the river by the ford. I never saw them again.'

'Easy, Will,' said Tucker. 'Easy now.'

I felt his arm slip round my shoulder, saw the shadow of his face draw close. The shivery presence moved up my spine like a rush of air. I opened my mouth to speak. Then remembered no more.

3

MURDER

I came round to find myself lying on the bed in the school medical room with the nurse sitting beside me. Standing behind her was an anxious-looking Mr Tucker. I felt groggy and confused and it took me a moment to remember what had happened.

Then the memory came back – the shivery presence, the shadows, the coldness, the voice that had spoken inside my head; and even through my mouth.

At least those things were gone for the moment. But I still felt scared. Mr Tucker smiled at me.

'You gave us a bit of a fright there, Will,' he said. 'Didn't he, Mrs Burton?'

'Certainly did,' said the nurse.

'What happened?' I asked her.

'You fainted by the school gate,' she said. 'Mr Tucker carried you here.'

Tucker gave me a slightly sheepish smile.

'I'm sorry I was a bit sarcastic to you up at the castle, Will,' he said. 'I didn't realise you were unwell.'

I said nothing.

'Now, Will,' said Mrs Burton. 'I wonder whether we ought to get your mum to come and collect you. A trip to the doctor might be a good idea. You look washed out and although I'm quite sure it's nothing serious, I think you ought to get a proper check-up. You can't have fainted for no reason. Did you wake up feeling poorly this morning?'

I looked away, unsure what to say. This was nothing to do with feeling poorly. But if I told people what had really happened, they'd think I was off my head. I didn't want to go to the doctor and I certainly didn't want to tell Mum.

She'd worry herself sick and probably tell Dad about it if he phoned.

Then he'd start worrying as well. And this was a day when he had talks with management. He'd need all his wits about him for that. I could ruin everything. It didn't bear thinking about. I looked back at Mrs Burton.

'You don't need to call Mum or anything. I'm OK now.'

'You don't look OK. You look really tired. Would you like to rest here for a bit? You don't have to go back to lessons just yet.'

'No, I'm OK. Honestly.'

I wasn't OK at all. I was still scared stiff. But I needed to be near my friends again.

'All right,' said Mrs Burton. 'We'll let you go to your lessons. But I want you to promise me you'll come straight back if you start to feel bad again. I'll give you a note to show your teachers in case you need to be excused at any point today.'

I left the medical room with Mr Tucker close beside me. The school was quiet, with lessons in progress, and it was good to feel the heat of the day back after the chill I had felt earlier.

'Are you sure you're all right, Will?' said Tucker.

'Yes, sir. Thank you.' I turned to set off down the corridor but to my surprise Tucker put out a hand to stop me.

'Will,' he said slowly, 'do you know what a ford is?'

'No, sir.'

'Hmm.' He looked down at me gravely. 'Then what did you mean when you talked about some people being killed and thrown in the river by the ford?'

I remembered the words that had somehow been spoken through my mouth. But I had no idea what they meant – or what a ford was.

'I don't know, sir,' I said.

Tucker watched me in silence for a moment, then said, 'A ford is a place where you can cross a river. You often have to wait for low water before you can do it but if there's no bridge or boat, it's often the only way across. There used to be a ford here in Totnes, but we don't need it any more, of course, with the bridges.'

He paused, stroking his chin.

'But when the Normans first came to Totnes, it would have been very important. The river was a different shape in those days too. It curved round at the bottom of town and the top bank reached some way up into what is now Fore Street. There were marshes as well. It was quite a different place.'

He smiled suddenly.

'But this isn't the time for another history lesson.' He handed me my unused worksheet on Totnes Castle. 'You might as well have this. You don't have to do any of the tasks but there's lots of information on the sheet that you might find interesting when you're feeling better. What lesson are you supposed to be in now?'

'French, sir.'

'Who with?'

'Mrs Soper.'

'OK. I'll just come with you and make sure she understands the situation.'

The class looked me over as I entered and there was an excited murmur round the room. I sat down at the back next to Cal and wished the others would stop looking at me.

'You OK?' Cal whispered. I saw Ellie mouthing me the same question from her seat at the front.

I shrugged, unable to answer them. Mr Tucker was talking to Mrs Soper in a low voice and she was nodding and looking my way. Then suddenly he was gone and she was facing the class again.

'Eh bien, tout le monde,' she began, and then continued as though nothing had happened.

I was grateful for that and also glad she didn't bother asking me any questions. She had obviously decided to let me just sit there. But when the class started the written exercise, she slipped over to my desk and leant down.

'All right, Will?' she said quietly.

'Yes, miss. Thanks.'

'You don't have to do this exercise if you don't want to. By all means have a go but if you don't feel like it, just leave it.'

'Thanks, miss.'

'Can I leave it too?' said Cal.

'Nice try, Calvin,' she said as she moved off.

I stared down at the desk. I hadn't even pulled my French books out of my bag. All I had before me was Tucker's worksheet on Totnes Castle. I saw a section entitled 'Background Information' and some of the words caught my eye.

Chapter 4

THE COMING
OF THE INVADERS

When the Normans arrived, Totnes was in the hands of the Saxons. It was a fortified town. There was a timber stockade all around it and the east gate down at the bottom of the high street really was a gate, not just an open archway like it is today.

But there was no stopping the Normans. They were a highly disciplined fighting force. They quickly took over the town.

To my horror, I felt the shivery presence move inside me again. I stiffened and looked around the room. I felt sure the others must have sensed the change in me. But no one looked my way, not even Cal scribbling next to me.

I listened for the voice and there it was speaking inside my head. I could feel it trying to break out through my mouth again. I pressed my lips tightly together but the voice just went on murmuring through my brain.

'We had no chance,' it said. 'Judhael was too strong.'

A shadow fell over the windows. The walls darkened. The scorching summer heat was swept away by a mist of cold air. Yet Cal and the others went on writing as though nothing had changed. My eye fell on more words.

The Normans spoke French. They would have given their instructions to the conquered Saxons through an interpreter.

I frowned. It seemed strange to be reading this in a French lesson. The voice spoke again and it was only with the greatest effort that I managed to keep the words from bursting out through my mouth. But I heard the voice mutter inside my head.

'They brought a man with them to give us Judhael's commands. A man who spoke our tongue. But he was not one of us. He was scum.'

My classmates had turned to shadows. The features of the room were slipping into darkness. I clutched the worksheet. It felt like all I had left of the world I had known.

'Eh bien!' Mrs Soper's voice rang out again. 'Vous avez fini?'

There was a bustle of noise around the room. The voice in my head faded and the figures and shapes of my world returned. Trembling, I looked down at Tucker's worksheet again.

The Norman commander in Totnes was called Judhael.

Judhael. The voice had used that name just a
moment ago. I clenched my fists. I couldn't take
any more of this. I stood up, glanced at Cal and
Ellie, then made my way to the front of the
class. The room fell silent as I approached Mrs
Soper. She smiled at me.

'Yes, Will?'

'Miss,' I said, 'I want to go home.'

Mum was
at the school
within minutes. She
took one look at me and
said we were going straight to
the doctor's. I shook my head. I
didn't want a check-up. I just wanted to go
home. I needed safe, familiar things around me
right now. She started to argue, then, when she
saw I was close to tears, she just put her arm
round me and took me out to the car.

She was calmer than I'd expected her to be.
She didn't force me to speak. She just drove me
home, gave me some soup, and let me go to
bed, which was all I wanted.

I said nothing about the strange things that had happened to me. I knew they'd only freak her out and besides, I didn't understand them myself. So I just said I was feeling shivery.

And that was true. The restless presence was still inside me.

I tried to ignore it and read more of Tucker's worksheet.

The Norman commander in Totnes was called Judhael. After the Battle of

Hastings in 1066 the Normans took over Saxon England. Judhael and his men marched into Totnes in the winter of 1067 and took over the town.

Though the Saxons outnumbered the Normans, they were unable to resist the fighting power of the invaders. Judhael immediately ordered a castle to be built in Totnes to act as a garrison for his troops and a power base for himself.

The voice spoke again through my lips.

'It wasn't Judhael who killed them. It was one of his men.'

Again I tried to ignore it and read on.

Nowadays the castle has stone walls but when it was first built, everything would have been made of timber.

There would have been a palisade and a watchtower up on the motte.

The bailey would have had another palisade and probably a couple of small towers with drawbridges, one leading out of town, the other leading into it.

The castle was a symbol of Norman power. It was intended to dominate the town and quell any thoughts of rebellion among the Saxons.

'It

was one of Judhael's men,' the voice said. 'I spit on him.'

I felt the shivery presence move again. Desperately I tried to hold on to the world I knew. But it was slipping away again.

I heard the sound of the front door, then Dad's worried voice saying, 'How is he?' to Mum. My heart sank. I hadn't realised she'd told him I was ill. She must have said I was in a really bad state or he'd never have come home with so much going on at work. I felt a rush of guilt at the trouble I was causing. Again the voice spoke through my lips.

'Come to the castle,' it said.

5

BURIED

Mum and Dad stayed close all day. They tried not to act over-concerned but it was obvious they were worried out of their minds. And when I saw myself in the mirror, I understood why. My face was white.

I tried to persuade Dad to go back to work but he wouldn't hear of it. He said there was nowhere else he wanted to be right now but here. Mum told me if there was no improvement by the morning, they were going to call out Doctor Willet. But for now they just wanted me to rest. So I stayed in bed and pretended to sleep.

At four o'clock Tucker rang to see how I was. I heard Mum take the call. She thanked him for his concern and told him I was resting.

Soon after that Odette came home from school. I heard her outside my room asking Dad if I could help her make a cat's cradle. She told him I'd promised her I would, which was true, and it made me feel even more guilty.

'He needs to rest, sweetheart,' I heard Dad say. 'But you can look round the door if you want and blow him a kiss.'

A moment later I saw the door open and Odette's wide eyes searching for mine. She caught them and grinned. I smiled back as best I could.

'I know,' I said. 'I've got one of my funny faces, haven't I?'

'Yes.'

'So how funny is it, then? On a scale of one to ten?'

This was a little complicated for her and I could see her frowning. So I said, 'Is it a very funny face? Or a very, very funny face?'

She thought for a moment.

'It's a very, very, very, very, very funny face,' she said eventually.

'Thanks a lot,' I said. 'Are you going to blow me that kiss now?'

She blew me a kiss and I blew one back. Outside the room I heard Dad murmur something, then Odette spoke again.

'Daddy says I've got to leave you alone now.'

'OK. See you later.' And I saw the door close again.

But she had not left me alone. The shivery presence was still with me. It had been silent for a while and I prayed it would remain so, but later that day, as dusk started to fall, it began speaking through my lips again.

'Come to the castle,' it said.

'Go away,' I muttered back.

'It's buried at the castle,' it said. 'We've got to find it. We've got to give it back. Come to the castle.'

'No,' I said firmly.

If there was one place I didn't want to see, it was the castle.

Yet even from my bed there was no avoiding the wretched thing. I could see it through my window. It stood there up at the top of town, the stone wall of the keep just visible in the failing light. A ghostly haze was now falling over it.

It was growing cold again too. Where before I had felt the warmth of June, now I sensed the chill of winter. I clutched the sheets, the duvet, the timber frame of my bed, anything that reminded me of the solid world I had known.

Because somehow it was slipping away again.

'Come to the castle,' the voice said through my lips. 'It's buried there. Come tonight. No one will see us in the darkness.'

'No,' I snarled.

'We've got to find it. We've got to give it back.'

'Give what back?'

'Come to the castle,' came the answer. 'Come tonight.'

I scrambled out of bed, my mind in turmoil. It was no good. I had to sort this thing out once and for all. I didn't know what I had to do. But whatever it was, I was determined to have some help.

I crept to the bedroom door, opened it and listened. Downstairs I could hear Mum, Dad and Odette talking in the kitchen. I could tell even without hearing their words that Mum and Dad were forcing themselves to sound cheerful for Odette's sake.

I hurried into Dad's study, picked up the phone and dialled. Cal's dad answered.

'Mr Lewsey?' I said. 'It's Will.'

'Will! Are you feeling better? Calvin says you had to go home today.'

'I'm...I'm fine, thanks. Is Cal there?'

'Sure. I'll get him.'

Cal was on a moment later.

'You OK?' he said.

'Sort of.'

'What does that mean?'

'Never mind. Listen, is your dad standing close by you?'

'No, he's gone downstairs. I'm on my own.'

'Good. Listen. Can you come somewhere with me later tonight? After your mum and dad have gone to bed? Only it's got to be a secret. No one must know.'

'Where do you want to go?'

'The castle.'

'Is this a joke?'

'No.'

'But what do you want to go there for?'

I hadn't the slightest idea. I remembered what the voice had said.

It's buried at the castle. We've got to find it. We've got to give it back.

'I've got to find something,' I said. 'That's all I can tell you.'

'What time do you want to meet?' said Cal.

'One in the morning.'

'You're kidding!'

'I'm not. There's got to be no chance of anyone seeing us.'

'I don't know if I want to do this,' said Cal. 'It sounds kind of scary.'

'Please, Cal.'

There was a long silence at the other end of the line.

'Please, Cal,' I said. 'I know this is crazy. But I really need you there.'

There was another silence. Then a hesitant, 'OK.'

6

THE CASTLE AT NIGHT

But Cal wasn't there when I arrived. I checked my watch. Just gone one o'clock. I stared at the sombre outline of the castle, then ran up the path to the locked entrance gate. To the right of it were two low walls.

They didn't look difficult to climb. I moved closer to the outer wall, hid in the shadows and waited for Cal. It felt eerie here but there was less chance of being seen if anyone came along Castle Street. Not that that was likely. The town was deserted.

Even so, I wished Cal would get here soon.
Maybe he'd found it hard to slip away. I hadn't
found it easy myself, though I didn't think
anyone heard me as I stole out the back door.
It was so cold now. It felt like wintertime. The
shivery presence spoke through my lips again.

'He killed them all. My father, my mother,
my little sister Osberga.'

I was shaking now, both with fear and
with the chill that hung upon the air. Who
was I? And who was this presence shivering
inside me?

'Who are you?'
I murmured, and the
answer came back
through my own lips.

'My name is Wulf.'

The word sounded strange.

'How old are you?' I asked, and again my own voice answered.

'Fourteen.'

'Who killed your father and mother and sister?'

'My enemy. I spit on him.'

'But who?'

'One of Judhael's knights. His name was Baldwin. He was a giant. He loved to kill.'

'What happened?'

'The Normans took over Totnes. Then Judhael spoke to my people through the interpreter. He told us we had to build a castle for him at the top of the town.

'But my father refused. Said he would never work for vermin. He tried to rally our people, make us stand up for ourselves and defy the Normans. He was that kind of man – brave, stubborn, honest. I loved him so much.

'But he should have kept his mouth shut. He should have known this cause was already lost. Judhael let him finish speaking, listened to what the interpreter said, then gave an order – and Baldwin stepped forward.'

The spirit boy called Wulf shuddered inside me, then spoke again through my voice.

'He towered over everyone. None of us had ever seen a man that tall. It wasn't human. I think even Judhael was frightened of him.

'I could see from my father's face that he knew he'd made a mistake. He ran over to me, slipped me his dagger in secret and said, "Avenge me if I'm killed". And then he tried to flee. But they caught him.'

The spirit boy shuddered again.

'They dragged him out through the east gate and down to the river. The whole town protested but there was nothing we could do. The Normans were too strong. Judhael watched from his horse, protected by his knights and by the soldiers.

'Then he spoke to us again through the interpreter. He said we had to witness what would happen to anyone who refused to build the castle for him.'

I felt my voice falter. But the words kept coming.

'Baldwin drew his sword and cut my father's throat in front of us. Then he dropped the body, strode over to Osberga and before I could shout a warning, sliced off her head with one blow. She was seven! She was just a little girl!

'He closed upon my mother. She shouted at me to run. I turned and bolted through the crowd. Behind me I heard her screams as Baldwin killed her. I went on running and somehow escaped into the woods outside Totnes. I never saw my family again. I found out later Baldwin had thrown their bodies in the river by the ford.'

I thought of Mum and Dad and Odette and felt a sudden, overwhelming pain.

'I hid in the woods,' my voice murmured on. 'It was winter. It was cold. I slept in a deserted peasant's cottage. I thought I would die. But I wanted to live. I wanted my revenge.

'My friends helped me. Caedmon found me first. He went back and told Elfleda where I was and she came with him after that. They were the best friends I could have had. They brought me food and warm clothing, and told me what was happening in Totnes. But I could see for myself.'

My voice was turning bitter like the night.

'Judhael had turned our people into slaves. He made them work every hour of the day to build his stinking castle. They had no time even to tend their own animals. I hid with Caedmon and Elfleda at the edge of the woods and watched the work go on.'

'Judhael had armed men everywhere and he gave our people no rest. Those who didn't work hard enough were handed over to Baldwin.'

There was a pause, then, 'They worked hard enough after he'd finished with them.'

My voice was no longer bitter. It was fierce with anger.

'My people had to do everything. They dug the ditches, carried the earth, built the great

mound. They cut the timber and put up the palisades. They built the watchtower and the stables, and the barracks and workshops and storerooms, and Judhael's precious hall.

'It took them two months, working every day in the freezing cold. And when it was done, Judhael made them swear an oath of allegiance before he would let them go back to their homes.'

I heard footsteps coming up Castle Street and drew back into the shadow of the wall. A moment later two figures appeared at the bottom of the path that led up to the entrance gate. I felt a rush of relief.

It was Cal – and he'd brought Ellie with him. They were looking nervously around them and clearly hadn't seen me.

'Here!' I called.

They stiffened, then Ellie pointed towards me.

'There he is!' she said.

They ran up and joined me.

'I wasn't expecting you,' I said to Ellie.

'Cal rang me,' she answered. 'Said you needed some moral support.'

'Do your parents know you're out?'

'Don't be stupid. And neither do Cal's. What's going on, Will?'

Again I remembered what the spirit boy had said.

It's buried at the castle. We've got to find it. We've got to give it back.

'I don't know,' I said. 'I've just...got to find something.'

'What?' said Ellie.

'I don't know.'

'Oh, great,' she said dryly. 'That'll help us a lot. And where are we supposed to look for this...this something?'

'In the castle grounds,' I said.

I saw them exchange glances, then Cal spoke.

'Listen, Will, I don't know if...you know...'
He glanced at Ellie, then back at me. 'I mean,
the castle's a really spooky place at night.'

'Can't you look tomorrow?' said Ellie. 'In
daylight?'

I shook my head. I knew it had to be now.
I could feel the spirit boy straining towards the
wall, tugging so hard he almost pulled me with
him. I didn't blame Cal and Ellie for being
scared. I was scared too. But I didn't want

them to come
in with me
against their will. I
saw the guilt on their faces
and quickly spoke again.

'It's OK, I didn't mean you to come in with
me. I just wanted you to hang around out here
in case there's any trouble.'

Ellie leant forward, her eyes dark and
earnest, and I sensed that she suspected the lie.
But all she said was, 'Don't go in, Will. Leave it
till daylight.'

'She's right,' said Cal. 'It can't be that
important, this thing you want to find.'

But I shook my head again. 'I've got to do it,'
I said.

Cal frowned, then pulled out a mobile phone. 'Well, if there's any trouble, I'm ringing for help.'

I picked up the spade I'd brought with me from home.

'So it's buried, then?' said Ellie. 'This thing you're looking for?'

'Yeah.'

'And do you know where exactly?'

I threw the spade over into the grounds, then glanced at her.

'I haven't got the faintest idea,' I said.

And before either of them could speak again, I turned and started to climb.

THE SHADOW WAKES

The moment I was in, I knew I was not alone.

It wasn't just the spirit boy called Wulf. It was something else, something that moved in countless places like swirls of darkness. I heard a voice speak. It was my own – yet it belonged to my strange companion.

'Hurry,' it said. 'We must find it before they get to us.'

'Who?' I asked.

There was no answer but I felt the shivery presence move inside me. And suddenly I was moving too. I did not know where I was going. I only knew that I was being led. I walked past the ticket hut and over the broad, grassy area of the bailey.

The air was colder than ever now, the sky almost black. I could hear sounds. I could hear laughter, singing, a blurry confusion of voices. I had heard voices like this around closing time at the pub down our road.

But this was no pub and these voices belonged to another century. I heard a clink of steel, a clump of boots, the neighing of horses. I moved on, led as before by the restless spirit boy. With every step I took, I felt my old world leaving me.

'Stay,' I murmured to it. 'Please stay.'

It clung on somehow, that world of Mum and Dad and Odette, and Cal and Ellie, and Mr Tucker and Mrs Burton, and the castle I had known – the castle that had once been so beautifully, reassuringly boring.

How I yearned for it to be boring again. But everything was changing now. I was walking from a world I loved into a world I had no wish to visit. My feet were no longer my own, and neither were my lips.

'Here,' they said. 'This is the place.'

I stopped and looked about me. Somehow I had wandered right round the base of the motte to the far side of the bailey. I looked up to the top of the mound, searching for a glimpse of the old stone walls.

But all I saw was black mist falling.

I felt my lips move again.

'Dig,' they said.

I started to dig in the soft earth at the foot of the motte. I was so cold now I could barely hold the spade and I was certain I could feel snow on my face. But I went on digging. And as I dug, words rushed out of me in a torrent, as though my companion had much to say and little time.

'It was at dusk one day when I saw my chance. There was a cart heading for the main gate of the castle. Caedmon and Elfleda tried to persuade me not to go in but I knew I had to. We ran up behind and I climbed underneath and clung between the wheels, while Caedmon and Elfleda talked to the driver to distract him. He didn't see me and neither did the sentries as the cart entered the castle.

'I felt so frightened without Caedmon and Elfleda there and my heart sank even further when I saw the drawbridge being pulled up after me. The only way out now would be through the other gate that led from the castle into the town itself. If they pulled up the drawbridge there too, I would have no escape at all.

'But I knew I had to go through with this, for my family's sake. I slipped out from under the cart, scurried across the bailey and hid in the hay store. No one saw me. A heavy snow started to fall and I heard the sound of singing from the great hall.'

I could hear singing too, and feel snow on my face. But I went on digging. More words poured out of me.

'I waited for hours, long into the night. The snow went on falling. It was growing heavier and heavier, and still the singing went on in the great hall. Then at last it stopped – and a moment later I saw my enemy.

'You could not miss a man that size. He had come from the hall with a crowd of other knights and they were drunk. They were laughing as they staggered through the snowstorm towards the steps that climbed up

to the watchtower. But Baldwin was a few
paces behind the rest.

'It was all I needed. I ran up, jumped on his
back and drove my father's dagger into his
neck. He clutched the air and fell with a great
shout. The others turned and came running.

'But by the time they reached him, I'd cut
his throat.'

I felt the spade touch something solid deep in the earth. Trembling, I reached down into the hole. My fingers closed round a slim, metal object. As they did so, I felt a shadowy form draw close.

More words rushed out of me. 'Give it back to them! They must know they are avenged! They will rest then!'

I pulled the object out and found myself holding a small, silver dagger. I knew at once whose it was – and what I had to do. I spoke urgently to the spirit boy.

'What happened to you? Tell me. I must know.'

'Darkness,' came the answer. 'Darkness…'

I closed my hand tight round the hilt and turned. Before me, framed against the mist, was a huge, unearthly figure. I stared up at it in dread.

'But he killed you,' I murmured. 'He cut your throat.'

It made no sound. It simply moved closer. The body lengthened and leaned down. I stared up at it in horror. There was no face at all. Only two specks of fire within a sea of black. I screamed out to Cal.

'Caedmon! Caedmon!'

But what was I saying? I was trying to call out to Cal.

'Caedmon! Caedmon!'

It was no use. I was no longer myself. My friend screamed back at last.

'Wulf! Run for it!'

And suddenly I was running.

8

FLIGHT

From all around me came shouts in the
hideous Norman tongue. I tore across the
bailey in the direction of the gate that led
into the town. But I could not see it. All I
saw was black mist and black figures,
clutching at me.

I ducked under swords, dodged under arms,
crawled under legs, wriggled and wrestled and
wrenched myself clear, and somehow ran on.
But where was the gate?

'Wulf! Wulf!'

It was a girl's voice and I recognised it at once.

'Elfleda!' I shouted back. 'Where are you?'

'Here!' came the answer.

She was somewhere to the right. I ran blindly on but now the mist was starting to clear.

I could see Judhael's hall before me. I could see the workshops, the barracks, the stables, the chapel. I could see the well. I could see the timber palisades and high above me the great wooden watchtower leering down at me from the top of the mound.

I could see snow
falling in thick,
heavy flakes.

There was the
gate – open and
with the
drawbridge down
– and there on the
other side were
Elfleda and Caedmon,
huddled against the inside of the town
wall, their backs to the snow.

But their eyes were on the gate. They saw me
at once and beckoned frantically. I darted
forward.

The sentries saw me too late and in the
darkness and confusion and driving snow I
slipped between them and stumbled onto the
drawbridge.

Caedmon and Elfleda rushed forward and
seized me by the arms.

'Come on!' shouted Elfleda. 'We've got to get
you away!'

We raced off into the town, skidding and
sliding on the slippery ground. From behind us
in the castle came the thunderous sounds of
pursuit.

We reached the top of the high street and
hared down it, past the pillory, past the
shambles and on towards the east gate.

On either side of us the thatch roofs were now white with snow.

I saw faces in the doorways, faces I knew and loved, faces too scared to speak. I saw Bertha and Harold and Walburga and Ethelbert, and little Hilda. They stared at me as if I were a ghost.

I could hear hooves behind us now. I could hear shouts. I could hear the rattle of swords and spurs. I could hear Baldwin's black spirit cursing me in my ear. It made me shiver as I ran. I had killed him once. Did I now have to kill him again?

I clutched my father's dagger and hurtled towards the east gate.

'You can't go this way!' shouted Caedmon. 'You've got to hide!'

'No!' I shouted back. 'I've got to get out of the town! There's something I've got to do!'

'But the east gate's locked!'

'I'm going to climb over the stockade!'

Without waiting for an answer, I cut past Alfred's house and raced down between the plots towards the stockade.

From Bede's land came the grunting of pigs and the smell of dung. I saw the old man in the doorway of his stable, warming his hands over a fire, his hair wet with snow. He said nothing as we tore past but his dog started to bark.

We reached the stockade, scrambled up to the walkway and looked back. A crowd had now formed in the high street, Normans and Saxons jostling together, but there was no doubt who was in control.

Judhael.

I could see him on his stallion, surrounded by mounted knights, barking orders to his soldiers. Then he saw me on the walkway. He pointed his sword and gave a shout.

At once men started to pour down between the plots towards the stockade. I glanced frantically over at the ground beyond. It wasn't a dangerous jump as long as it was done right. But it had to be now. There was no time to waste.

I turned to my friends. 'Go back to your homes,' I muttered. 'It's me the Normans want.'

And without looking back, I climbed over the edge of the stockade and let myself fall. I landed at the base, rolled into the ditch and scrambled up the other side. To my dismay, Caedmon and Elfleda had jumped too, and were still with me.

'You mustn't come any further,' I said. 'You have a chance to live.'

'But where are you going?' said Elfleda.

I stared down at the dagger, still tight in my hand.

'To the river,' I said. 'But I've got to do this on my own.' I reached out and touched each one on the cheek. 'I'll never forget you,' I said.

And then I ran.

9

Vengeance
and Death

The snow was driving so hard into my face I could barely see where I was going. I blundered on somehow towards the river. From behind me in the town came shouts and commotion.

But louder than all of these was the whispering curse of my enemy, close to my ear. I tightened my grip round the hilt of my father's dagger and plunged on. Then I heard a loud groan behind me. I knew at once what it was.

They were opening the east gate.

In spite of my haste, I stopped and looked back. And there they were: Judhael on his stallion, his mounted knights, his swordsmen, spearmen, archers. He had turned all his men out.

I stared at them. Could this really be for me? Did they think I was the start of a rebellion? Or was it just a show of strength to the people of Totnes to let them see what would happen to anyone who defied Norman authority?

Even a boy of fourteen.

They came hurtling down the slope. I turned and ran towards the river. I would not stop now. I would give my father back his dagger. I would show my family I had avenged them. I would let them rest again. And I would join them soon.

The sound of the
hooves grew louder, louder.
I drove myself on towards the
river. There it was, just ahead, the
water flowing past me, dark and
cold. I heard the snorting of horses, the
drawing of swords. I stumbled into the
shallows, flung back my arm and made to
throw the dagger into the stream.

Before I could do so, something hard drove
into the back of my head.

I fell face down in the icy water, panic
flooding through me. I still held the dagger but
I had to give it back. I could feel my father's
spirit calling me in the water. I could feel my
mother's spirit, and Osberga's spirit. I struggled
to my feet and made to throw the dagger again.

Once more I was knocked down into the
shallows. Once more I clutched the dagger tight

and struggled to my feet. I had to throw it
before they killed me. They must not take it.
I saw shadows close around me, the shadows
of horses, the shadows of mounted knights,
the shadows of soldiers lining the shore.

Again I made to throw the dagger. Again the hard thing struck me in the head. And this time I saw what it was. It was Judhael's boot. I fell once more into the freezing water and still – somehow – held on to the dagger and struggled to the surface again.

This time, when I came up, I saw the knights circling me, their horses throwing up clouds of spray. Beyond them, soldiers lined the bank, some watching me, but most of them facing the townsfolk and braced for an attack.

But my people had not come to attack. I knew that well enough. They had come to see me die. What could they do against such overwhelming force? I stared at them all, Caedmon and Elfleda amongst them, and knew I was seeing them for the last time.

With a scream at Judhael, I turned and threw the dagger far out into the river. It fell without a splash and vanished as though it had never been. From deep in the water came a strange, soft sound. I swear it was a sigh.

The boot struck me again. I fell into the shallows and this time did not rise. I prayed that the end would be quick – a spear-thrust, a sword-thrust – but hands were twisting me by the hair, hauling my head above the surface of the water.

I stared up through the falling snow with all the defiance I could manage and saw two soldiers holding me for their lord to see.

And Judhael rode forward and looked down. And his mounted knights looked down. And those around him looked down. And far behind them all, high up above the town, the hateful watchtower of the castle looked down too. Even the snow could not brighten it.

But it was not the darkest thing I saw.

Something else was moving towards me, something I feared even more than death. It loomed closer as I waited, shivering, for the end, a huge, black shadow of pure evil. It was not a man. It was what was left of a man. But it was enough to fill the final seconds of my life with terror.

I heard a command from Judhael, then the hands tightened round my hair and pushed my head back into the water – and this time held it down.

10

THE MISSING DAGGER

I heard Caedmon call my name.

'Will! Will!'

I opened my eyes to find myself lying on something hard and staring up at the night sky. It was black – but there was no snow, and the air was warm. Caedmon's voice came again.

'Will!'

I could hear him clearly. He was somewhere near. But he was getting my name wrong.

'Wulf,' I murmured. 'I'm....'

'Will!' A girl's voice this time, a girl I knew. It sounded like Elfleda. And yet...it was Ellie.

Where was I? Who was I?

Hands were sliding under my back and neck. I felt myself being picked up. I looked to the side and saw Dad holding me in his arms. Mum and Odette were close by, and just behind them, Ellie and Cal. All had drawn, anxious faces.

Tears rushed upon me at the sight of them, tears of pain, tears of confusion, tears of relief.

'It's all right, Will.' Dad pulled me closer. 'It's all right. I've got you.'

I went on crying, my arms locked around him. His body felt firm and strong and alive. I wasn't imagining this. He was here. He was really here, just as Mum and Odette and Cal and Ellie were really here. But what had happened? I stopped crying and looked around me.

I was in Fore Street near the bottom of town, just outside The Lord Nelson pub. The shops and buildings of Totnes were dark and silent, though I could hear the faint sound of a car moving somewhere up in The Narrows. I gripped Dad's arm.

'Snowing,' I muttered. 'Why isn't it snowing?'

'It's June, Will,' said Dad. 'That's why. Can you stand?'

'Yeah.'

He put me down and I stood there on the pavement, trying to see the shapes of the world I had come from. But they were no longer there.

'It was snowing,' I said. 'It was...'

I stopped, seeing the confusion on their faces. Mum spoke, gently.

'You're going to be fine, Will.'

'But – '

'Let's get you home,' she said. 'It's too late to be out, especially for Odette. We wouldn't have brought her only we couldn't leave her at home on her own. Come on.'

'Wait!' I stared from face to face. 'What...what happened?'

'I was hoping you might tell us,' said Dad. He frowned. 'Cal phoned us on his mobile. Told us you were racing down the high street towards the bottom of town. We got here as quickly as we could.'

'You were ages in the castle,' said Cal. 'We were getting really scared. I was just trying to pluck up courage to climb in and look for you when you came running towards the gate.'

'You looked terrified,' said Ellie. 'You scrambled over the walls by the entrance gate –'

'I didn't,' I said. 'I ran across the drawbridge.'

She watched me for a moment in obvious bewilderment, then shrugged.

'Whatever. Anyway, you shot off up the hill and then went charging down the high street. I've never seen you run so fast. It was like you had an army chasing after you or something. Cal rang your dad on the mobile, then we belted off after you. You ran through the archway of the east gate – '

'I didn't!' I said. 'I had to climb over the stockade!'

Again she looked at me in bewilderment. Mum gave my hand a squeeze.

'Whatever you did, Will,' she said, 'you ended up here. We found you lying in the middle of the road, writhing about as though you were struggling with someone.'

I remembered the hands forcing me down. I remembered the black face pressed against my own as the water closed over me. Yet the river was a couple of hundred yards further down from here. You couldn't even see it from where I was standing. It was on the other side of the roundabout, hidden by buildings and the curve of Totnes Bridge.

I started to walk down Fore Street, searching
the ground. Dad caught me up at once and
took me by the arm.

'Will,' he said. 'Enough now. Come home.'

'I just –'

'Come home, lad. You need to rest.'

'Dad, please!' I looked round at him. 'I've got to do this.'

He frowned, then reluctantly let go of my arm. I carried on down Fore Street, scanning the ground as before. The others followed.

'What are you looking for?' said Mum warily.

I said nothing. I knew they thought I was mad. And maybe I was. Moments ago I had been in the shallows of the river; now I was walking down the street. Then I remembered something Tucker had said about how the shape of the river had changed, how it had come up much higher at the time of the Norman invasion.

Had it reached up to the place where Mum and Dad and the others had just found me? I walked down as far as the roundabout, searching for the weapon that had taken a man's life.

There was no sign of it. I stopped and looked back up the hill. Then suddenly I realised that just as I could not see the river from here, nor could I see the castle. It was hidden behind the buildings and the high arch of the east gate.

But I didn't need to see the castle. I knew what it would be like now. It would be made of stone again. The timber watchtower, the drawbridges, the palisades – all the things that I had seen would be gone, just as the stockade round the town was now gone.

Had this really been imagination?

On an impulse, I raised my right hand under the glow of a streetlamp. And there, in the palm, was the fading imprint of something I had gripped with all my strength.

The hilt of a dagger.

I turned to show my hand to the others but before I could do so, someone took it. I looked down and saw Odette standing there, smiling up at me. I smiled back and gave her hand a squeeze.

'So have I still got a funny face?' I said.

'A bit,' she answered. 'But not as funny as it was before.'

And I smiled at her again.

A shiver moved over my body, round and round, whirling like a breeze, turning me back

towards the bridge. Still holding Odette by the hand, I walked on towards the river – then stopped.

There, on the bridge, was the figure of a boy.

A boy about my age, my height, and somehow so like me I could have been staring at myself, though his strange, scrawny clothes came from a century long before mine. I heard Odette speak.

'What are you looking at, Will?'

'Can't you see?' I said.

'See what?'

'The boy.'

'What boy?'

I said no more. I just squeezed her hand again and went on watching the boy. He stared at me for a few moments, his face calm and still.

Then slowly disappeared.

11

RETURN TO THE CASTLE

I never told the others what really happened. I knew they'd never believe me. But I needn't have worried. They didn't push me to say anything. They just closed around me like a big warm glove. I felt closer to them than I had ever done before.

But I was changed.

On the surface I was getting better. But deep inside me some part of Wulf was still there. Life went on. Dad went back to work and to the dispute with management. Mum busied about the house. She kept me off school for a few days so that she could keep an eye on me.

Odette refused to leave my side so Mum kept her at home too. It turned out to be good for both of us. Spending hours making cat's cradles with Odette was the best therapy either of us could have had.

But I still wasn't right. I could hardly bear to let any of the family out of my sight. If Mum went to the shops or Odette ran into the garden, I couldn't relax until I saw them safely back. And if Dad was a few minutes late from work, I started to panic.

I saw a great sword rising. I saw it swinging through the air. I saw it cutting, cutting, cutting. I saw bodies in the river.

Then one evening the front door opened and there was a great shout from Dad.

'It's over! It's over! There's to be no strike! And Will's got a visitor!'

It was Tucker. He'd arrived at the same time as Dad. Mum brought out the ginger cake and made some tea. We sat in the kitchen and talked. Dad looked exhausted, but he was jubilant too. Management had agreed terms. There was to be no strike. Mr Tucker caught my eye.

'You must be proud of your old dad,' he said.

'I am,' I answered. Yet even as I spoke, I found my thoughts drifting to another man. A man who had paid too high a price for what was right. And a boy who had paid just as dearly for his revenge. I wondered – what price was I now paying for that same revenge?

Then Tucker spoke again.

'Will, I was wondering if you felt like coming with me to the castle tomorrow morning.'

There was nothing I wanted less. The mere thought of that ancient site still scared the life out of me. Yet for some reason I knew I had to go. If only to prove to myself that I could face it.

And when I went, I found it a strangely tranquil place. The moment I entered, I knew the darkness was gone. I'd been having nightmares of Judhael and his men, especially Baldwin, but now, as we climbed the steps to the old castle keep, I felt some of the fear slip away.

'Actually,' said Tucker, wheezing with exertion as we neared the top, 'I've got a bit of a soft spot for the Normans. I don't think they were such a bad lot after all. No worse than any other conquering power probably. They'd have had their bullies and their bad guys, of course. But they had to be ruthless. They were so heavily outnumbered. And Judhael did a lot of good things in Totnes. He founded a priory here. Did you know that?'

We reached the keep and wandered round it for a while. Then we climbed up to the wall walk and gazed over Totnes. It felt good to have no shivery presence inside me this time.

'No,' Tucker went on, 'I reckon the Normans were all right. And they left us lots of good things. Names for a start.'

'Names?'

'Oh, yeah.'

I shouldn't have encouraged him. He was straight back on his hobbyhorse. He told me that names like Ellie and Cal and Odette were based on Norman names. And his own name, Guy, was a Norman name. And so were Mum's and Dad's names – Valerie and Robert. And as for Will, that was probably the most famous Norman name of all.

Yet in spite of that, I felt only Saxon blood running through me.

I saw Tucker watching me strangely. Then, in an unusually hesitant voice, he said, 'Will, there's something I want to show you.'

I don't know why but I suddenly started to feel uneasy again. Maybe it was Tucker's hesitant voice. Or his somewhat awkward manner. He seemed almost unsure of himself. He led me back down to the bailey and round the base of the motte, then stopped.

And there in the place I had hoped we would avoid were the clear signs of the hole I had dug – except that it was now much deeper, much wider. I looked round and saw Tucker watching me again. Then he reached into his pocket and pulled out a piece of paper.

'This might interest you,' he said. 'It's from The Totnes Times.'

I took the paper from him and unfolded it. But before I could read it, a picture flashed into my mind. A picture I had seen before. A picture I would never forget.

I saw a boy's face. I saw a man lying dead.

I saw blood on snow.

Then the picture cleared and the words slipped into focus. I started to read.

GRISLY DISCOVERY AT TOTNES CASTLE

Staff arriving to open the castle on the morning of 10th June were astonished to find a spade lying next to a hole several feet deep at the base of the motte. It is not known who dug this hole and at first it appeared to be empty. Closer examination, however, revealed a human bone half-hidden in the earth at the bottom. Further excavation has now been carried out and two complete skeletons have been discovered. One is of a small boy around fourteen years of age. The other is of a man – over seven foot tall.